# THE BOLD, BAD BOYS!

### and other stories

**CLIVEDEN PRESS**

Published in Great Britain in 1994 by Cliveden Press,
an imprint of Egmont Publishing Limited, Egmont House,
PO Box 111, Great Ducie Street, Manchester M60 3BL.
Printed in Finland

ISBN 0 7498 2037 3

# *Enid Blyton*

Enid Blyton was born in London in 1897. Her childhood was spent in Beckenham, Kent, and as a child she began to write poems, stories and plays. She trained to be a teacher but she devoted her whole life to being a children's author. Her first book was a collection of poems for children, published in 1922. In 1926 she began to write a weekly magazine for children called *Sunny Stories*, and it was here that many of her most popular stories and characters first appeared. The magazine was immensely popular and in 1953 it became *The Enid Blyton Magazine*.

She wrote more than 600 books for children and many of her most popular series are still published all over the world. Her books have been translated into over 30 languages. Enid Blyton died in 1968.

# Contents

# Well really, Clockwork Mouse!

The clockwork mouse was a good little thing till the day he discovered the old paint-box at the back of the toy cupboard.

"What's this?" he asked the big doll.

"A paint-box, silly," said the big doll. "You get a paint-brush and dip it into water, then you dab it on to one of those paints – and you can paint all sorts of colours with the brush! Leave it alone. It isn't yours."

But the clockwork mouse didn't leave it alone. He thought it was a wonderful thing. You could paint colours everywhere by just dabbing a wet brush on those square coloured slabs in the tin box!

He found a brush. He couldn't find any water so he thought he would lick

the brush to make it wet. And, dear me, when he dabbed the wet brush on to a red paint, and then dabbed the brush on to the wall of the toy cupboard, he made a bright red patch.

"It's marvellous!" thought the clockwork mouse, and stopped being a good little thing from that very moment! He didn't tell anyone, though. He wanted to keep it a secret.

Peculiar things began to happen in the playroom among the toys.

One day everyone stared hard at the big doll, who had been sound asleep and had just woken up.

"What's the matter? Why are you staring?" she asked.

"Your cheeks are blue instead of red," said the baby doll. "You look peculiar. Do you feel ill?"

And then the teddy bear looked down at himself the next day and found that his tummy was bright red. How very, very strange. It had been a nice brown furry tummy, and now it was red.

Perhaps he was ill, too? He felt most alarmed.

"What's happening?" said the toys. "We keep waking up with something strange about us. Are we going to be ill? Is it catching?"

The clockwork mouse giggled to himself in his corner. This was funny. He kept wanting to laugh all the time when he looked at the big doll's blue cheeks and the teddy bear's red tummy.

The next day everyone was staring in horror at the pink rabbit. His pink face was white! Yes, white all over, and he looked really frightening.

"What's the matter?" he said. "Am I blue or something?"

"Your pink face is white," said the teddy bear. "It looks dreadful. What *can* be happening? Is it an illness, or a bad spell, or what?"

The clockwork mouse was thoroughly enjoying himself. He kept licking his brush and getting more and more colours out of the wonderful paint-box.

He was very clever at painting the toys while they slept. Nobody guessed what was happening at all.

Soon the dolls' house had purple walls instead of cream. They looked dreadful. Then the big doll's shoes appeared in pink and yellow instead of white, and the little doll's hat became bright red instead of pale blue. It was all very puzzling.

The sailor doll found that his shoes were brilliant orange one morning, and when he bent down to look at them everyone shouted loudly, "The top of your head is green! It's green! It's very green indeed!"

Well, it wasn't long before everyone had something peculiar about them except the clockwork mouse. The toys expected him to appear in red or blue or yellow one day, but he didn't. He just remained grey with a nice long tail.

Goodness knows what would have happened next if the clockwork mouse hadn't suddenly felt ill. He had been planning to paint the playroom walls with blue and orange, but when he dipped his brush into his mouth to wet it, as usual, he suddenly felt very sick.

He went and lay down in a corner of the empty brick-box, feeling very sorry for himself. The pink rabbit came up to him, with his face still very white indeed. "What's the matter?" he said. "Do you feel ill?"

"Yes, very," said the clockwork mouse. "Very, very."

The toys talked together. They were upset. "Better look at his tongue," said the sailor doll. "That's the first thing that doctors do when anyone is ill."

"Put out your tongue and let us see it," said the teddy bear to the mouse. So he put out his tongue. The toys gave loud screams. It was all the colours of the rainbow!

"It's pink and yellow and blue and green and purple and white . . ." began the sailor doll, in horror. "What illness has he got? What a terrible tongue!"

The big doll stared hard at the clockwork mouse's tongue. Then she pointed her finger at him.

"You bad, naughty, wicked little mouse!" she said. "It's *you* that has given me blue cheeks, and given the rabbit a white face, and the bear a red tummy. You've been using that paint-box! I know you have!"

The clockwork mouse gave a little squeak. "I feel ill. I feel ill."

"And it serves you right!" said the big doll. "Do you know why you feel ill? Because you've been putting that paint-brush into your mouth with all the paint on it, instead of using water as I told you. Now you've poisoned yourself with the paint. It serves you right."

The mouse began to cry. He was frightened. "I'm very sorry. It was a joke. I'm poisoned. Oh, what shall I do?"

"You can just wait till we've all washed off the paint you dabbed on us," said the big doll. "Thank goodness we know what it is! Come along to the basin, everyone, and we'll soon look ourselves again."

Well, the teddy got rid of his red tummy, the rabbit's face came pink again, the sailor doll washed off the green on the top of his head, and the big doll no longer had blue cheeks. They all felt much more cheerful when they had washed off the paint.

"It was naughty of him – but it was a bit funny, too," said the teddy bear. "No wonder I kept hearing him giggling away in his corner. He's always been such a good, quiet little thing. Who would have thought he could be such a mischief?"

"I think we'll forgive him," said the rabbit. "He's feeling very sorry for himself. We'll give him some water to drink to wash the paint off his tongue. Then he'll feel better."

He did, of course, and now he's quite all right again. But would you have thought a clockwork mouse could ever have played such a trick?

# The quarrelsome bears

There were once two bears who lived in a little yellow cottage in Toy Village. Teddy was a brown bear and Bruiny was a blue one. And how they quarrelled! Really, you should have heard them!

"That's my handkerchief you are using!" said Teddy.

"Indeed it's not!" said Bruiny.

"I tell you it *is*," said Teddy.

"And I tell you it's not!" said Bruiny.

"Don't keep telling me fibs," said Teddy.

"Well, don't you either," said Bruiny.

That was the sort of quarrel they had every single day. Silly, wasn't it? Especially as they both had more handkerchiefs than they needed.

One afternoon they dressed themselves in their best coats and ties to go to a party. They did look nice. Teddy tied Bruiny's bow and Bruiny tied Teddy's. Then they took their new hats and went to the door.

And it was raining! Not just raining quietly, but coming down angrily and fiercely – pitterpatterpitterpatterpitterpatter, without a single stop.

"Goodness! Look at that!" said Teddy. "We must take our umbrella."

They had a big red umbrella between them, and it was really a very fine one indeed. Teddy looked for it in the umbrella-stand. It wasn't there.

"What have you done with the umbrella, Bruiny?" asked Teddy.

"Nothing at all," said Bruiny, at once. "What do you suppose I've done with it? Used it to stir my tea with?"

"Don't be silly," said Teddy. "That umbrella was there yesterday. You must have taken it out."

"I did not," said Bruiny. "You must have taken it yourself."

"I haven't been out for two days," said Teddy. "What do you think I'd want with an umbrella indoors?"

"Oh, you might use it to smack the cat with," said Bruiny unkindly.

"Oh! As if I would smack our dear old cat with an umbrella!" cried Teddy angrily.

"Well – perhaps you used it to poke the fire," said Bruiny.

"And perhaps *you* used it to scrub the floor!" cried Teddy. "I can think of silly things too. No, it's no good, Bruiny. You took that umbrella for something, and you might just as well try and remember what you did with it and where you put it. Hurry, now, or we'll be late for the party."

"I tell you, Teddy, I haven't had the umbrella and I don't know where it is," said Bruiny. "It would be a good thing if *you* thought a little and found out where you had hidden it."

"I don't hide umbrellas," said Teddy.

"Well, you once hid the cat in the cupboard and it jumped out at me," said Bruiny.

"That was just a joke," said Teddy. "I shouldn't hide our umbrella in the cupboard, because it wouldn't jump out at you."

"But you'd like it to, I suppose?" cried Bruiny, getting crosser and crosser.

"Yes, I'd love to see an umbrella jump out at you!" shouted Teddy, getting angry too.

"You're a bad teddy bear!" said Bruiny, and he pulled Teddy's bow undone.

"Don't!" cried Teddy. He caught hold of Bruiny's coat, meaning to give him a good shaking. But he shook too hard and the coat tore in half!

"Oh! Oh! Look at that!" wailed Bruiny. "I'll jump on your hat for tearing my coat!"

And before Teddy could stop him, Bruiny had thrown his new hat on the floor and jumped on it. It was quite spoilt!

Then they both went mad. They tore each other's ties off. They threw both hats out of the window. They even threw each other's handkerchiefs into the waste-paper basket!

And in the middle of all this there came a knocking at the door! Bruiny went to open it, panting and torn. Outside stood Mrs Field-Mouse with all her little family. They were on their way to the party, each mouse under its own tiny umbrella.

"Goodness me! What's all the noise about?" asked Mrs Field-Mouse severely. "I knocked three times before you heard me."

"Well, Mrs Field-Mouse," said Bruiny, "Teddy has taken our umbrella and doesn't know where he put it."

"Oh, you fibber!" cried Teddy. "It's Bruiny that must have taken it, Mrs Field-Mouse. We've only got one, and it's raining, and we wanted it to go to the party."

"Dear me!" said Mrs Field-Mouse.

"What have *you* come for?" asked Bruiny.

"Well, I came to give you back your big red umbrella," said Mrs Field-Mouse with a laugh. "I suppose you forgot that you both kindly said I might have it yesterday to go home with my little family, because it was big enough to shelter them all. I promised to bring it back today. Here it is. I'm sorry you should have quarrelled about it."

She stood it in the hall-stand and then went off to the party with her little family. How they squealed when they heard the joke!

"Well, I never," said Bruiny, looking at the umbrella. "So you didn't take it, Teddy."

"And you didn't either," said Teddy. "Oh dear, how silly we are! We've got our umbrella – but we've torn our suits and ties and spoilt our hats, so we can't possibly go to the party after all."

"I beg your pardon, Teddy," said Bruiny in a small voice. "I'll make you some cocoa for tea."

"And I beg your pardon, too," said Teddy. "I'll make you some toast for tea. We'll never quarrel again!"

But they did quarrel, and do you know why? It was because Teddy couldn't find the toasting-fork, so he toasted the bread on the end of the red umbrella! Bruiny was so angry, because he said the toast tasted of mud!

Well, well, well! You can't please everybody, can you?

## The rabbit who lost his tail

In the playroom cupboard with all the other toys lived Bun the soft rabbit. He was dressed in an orange tunic and green shorts, and his tail stuck out behind. It was a funny little tail, very short and fluffy, just like a real rabbit's.

Bun often played with Mollie, his mistress. She used to take him into the garden with her, and he sat on a little wooden chair and pretended to have tea. He was a very happy little rabbit.

One day a pixie climbed in at the window and gave Bun a letter. It had a crown printed on the back, so Bun knew that it had come from a King or Queen. He was very excited and his

paws trembled when they tried to undo the envelope.

All the other toys crowded round to see what the letter inside was. Bun unfolded it and read it out loud. It was from the King of Fairyland!

DEAR BUN,
I am having a party under the old beech tree on Wednesday night at moonrise. Please come if you can.
Love from
THE KING OF FAIRYLAND.

Bun danced for joy. He had always wanted to go to a pixie party, but toys didn't very often get asked.

"Wednesday!" he said. "That's two days away. Oh, how can I wait?"

Bun was very happy all that day – but the next day something dreadful happened. He lost his tail!

Mollie had taken him out into the garden to play with him and the little boy next door came to play too. But he was rather rough with Bun, and to make Mollie laugh he held the little rabbit up by his tail.

But Mollie didn't laugh. She snatched Bun away from the little boy and scolded him.

"That's not funny!" she said. "You'll hurt Bun. You're a nasty little boy and I don't want to play with you any more."

Then the two began to quarrel, and soon they were shouting at each other loudly. Mother came out and sent the little boy away. Then she took Mollie indoors.

All that day Bun lay out on the grass. The rain came and made him wet. Then suddenly Mollie remembered him and ran out to fetch him. She sat him in front of the playroom fire to dry, and there he stayed in the warm until Mollie went to bed.

Then, when the playroom was empty and quiet, all the other toys crept round Bun to hear what had happened. He told them all about the little boy who held him up by the tail and the toys exclaimed in horror.

Then suddenly the bear gave a squeak.

"Ooh, Bun!" he said. "Where *is* your tail?"

Then all the toys looked at Bun's back, and sure enough his tail was gone. He had no tail at all.

He *was* upset! He turned his head round to look at the place where his tail wasn't, and the tears came into his eyes.

"What shall I do?" he wept. "I can't go to a pixie party without a tail, I really can't. Why, I should feel only half-dressed. Oh, whatever shall I do?"

The toys looked at one another and thought hard.

"I'll run out into the garden and see if I can find your tail for you," said the clockwork clown. "If someone will wind me up, I can easily get there and back."

The teddy bear wound him up and the clockwork clown ran out of the room and down the passage that led to the garden. He hunted everywhere about the grass for Bun's tail, but he couldn't find it. At last he didn't dare to hunt any longer for he was afraid his clockwork would run down, and then he wouldn't be able to get back to the playroom.

"Well," said the toys, when he went back to them, "did you find it?"

"No," said the clown, "it isn't there."

Then Bun wept more loudly than ever, and all the toys looked at one another and thought hard again.

"Couldn't one of you lend me a tail?" asked Bun, at last.

"I haven't got one or I would with pleasure," said the teddy bear.

"What about the baby lamb that lives in the toy stable?" cried the clown. "He has a fine long tail, and I am sure he would lend it to you."

"But wouldn't I look funny with a very long tail?" asked Bun. "My own was so short."

"Oh, a long tail is better than nothing," said the teddy, and all the toys agreed. So they went to fetch the baby lamb from the stable and told him what they wanted. He didn't like parting with his tail at first, but when the clown told him all about the wonderful pixie party that Bun had been invited to, he said yes, he would lend his tail just for that night.

"It's only pinned on," he said, "so Bun can quite easily unpin it and put it on himself."

"Well, I'll borrow it tomorrow, and thank you very much," said Bun, happily. Then all the toys went to sleep, and the playroom was quiet.

The next night the toys fetched the lamb again, and the clown unpinned his tail. It was very long, soft and woolly and felt lovely and warm. Bun turned his back to the clown, and in a trice it was neatly pinned on.

"Ooh, Bun!" said the teddy bear, "you do look fine! A long tail suits you much better than a short one. Everyone will look at you and admire you."

Bun felt very happy. He took his invitation card, said goodbye to the toys and set off to the big beech tree. The moon was just rising, and as he came near the tree he could see crowds of pixies and elves there.

Bun wondered if Tiptoe, the elf who lived in the foxglove bed, was going to the party too. He was very fond of Tiptoe, and he had often wished that she would marry him and live with him in the playroom. But he had never dared to ask her, for she was very lovely.

Suddenly he saw her. She ran up to him and tweaked one of his big ears.

"Hello, Bun!" she said. "I'm so glad you're going to the party."

"Will you dance with me?" asked Bun, in delight.

"Yes," said Tiptoe, and then she sneezed three times.

"Oh dear, you haven't got a cold, have you?" asked Bun in alarm. "What a thin dress you have on, Tiptoe, and the wind is so cold too."

"Yes, I ought to have put on something warmer," said Tiptoe, and she shivered, "but it's too late now. Perhaps I shall get warm dancing."

The party soon began. The band struck up a merry tune, and all the pixies and elves began to dance. The King and Queen sat on two toadstool thrones, and clapped when each dance was finished.

Bun enjoyed himself very much, because everyone admired his tail.

"What a beautiful tail!" they said. "You *are* a lucky rabbit to have a tail like that! How nice you look! Will you dance with us?"

So Bun danced every single dance, and was so happy that his ears turned bright red inside. But he liked dancing best with Tiptoe. He was worried about her because she did sneeze so, and he

felt certain she would get a very bad cold, and be ill.

Suddenly the Queen heard Tiptoe sneezing and she called her to the throne.

"Why didn't you put on a warmer dress?" she said. "You really must go home, Tiptoe, for you will get a terrible cold."

"Oh, please, Your Majesty, do let me stay!" said poor Tiptoe. "A-tishoo, a-tishoo!"

Then a wonderful idea came to Bun. He ran up to the Queen and bowed.

"I can lend Tiptoe a fur to put round her neck," he said. "Would you let her stay if she wears a fur, Your Majesty?"

"Certainly," said the Queen. "But where is the fur?"

"Here!" said Bun, and he unpinned the long woolly lamb's tail! He put it around Tiptoe's neck, and there she was, as warm as toast, and as pretty as a picture.

How all the elves and pixies cheered! They knew that Bun was proud of his long tail and felt very odd without it, and they thought it was very kind and unselfish of him to lend it to Tiptoe and go without it himself.

After that Bun was more of a hero than ever. All the elves wanted to dance with him, but he danced all the rest of the time with Tiptoe, who had stopped sneezing and felt quite warm with the lamb's tail round her neck.

"I'll see you home," said Bun, after the party. "You can wear the fur all the way to the foxglove bed, and when you're nice and warm at home, you can give me the tail to take back to the baby lamb, who lent it to me. I lost my own tail."

"How sad for you!" said Tiptoe. "But what a good thing for me, because if you hadn't lost your own tail you wouldn't have been able to lend me this fur, and I should have had to go home early! Tomorrow I'll have a good hunt for your own tail, Bun. Now, goodnight, and thank you for your kindness."

Bun said goodnight and ran home very happy. He told all the toys what had happened and the baby lamb was very pleased when he heard how useful his tail had been. The teddy bear pinned it on to his back again, and then all the toys settled themselves to sleep.

Next evening there came a tapping at the playroom window and who should it be but Tiptoe!

"Bun!" she called. "Bun! Come quickly! I've found your tail!"

Bun ran to the window and opened it. There was Tiptoe, and in her hand was Bun's own little short tail.

"Where did you find it?" he asked, in delight.

"A worm had pulled it down into his hole," said Tiptoe. "I took it away from him and washed it. Now it is dry and clean, and if you come with me I'll sew it on so tightly for you that you will never lose it again."

So Bun went to the foxglove bed with Tiptoe and she sewed his tail on for him again with a hundred stitches so that it was very firm indeed.

"You are the dearest elf I ever saw!" said Bun. "I do wish you would marry me, Tiptoe. We could live in the dolls' house, and be very happy together."

"Ooh, let's!" said Tiptoe, and she flung her arms round Bun and hugged him. He had never been so happy in all his life.

They moved into the dolls' house, and, oh, what a merry time they had! They gave parties every night, and Tiptoe learnt to cook lovely cakes on the little tin stove in the kitchen. And they *always* ask the baby lamb to their parties, because if it hadn't been for his long woolly tail Bun and Tiptoe would never have got married!

## Paddy the puppy

Alan was staying with his Auntie Betty and his cousin Jenny. He liked it very much except that Auntie Betty was much stricter than his own mother!

She made him wipe his feet properly and hang up his things as soon as he took them off. "If you throw them down on the floor again you won't have any cake for tea!" she told him – and when he forgot, she kept her word and he *didn't* have cake for tea! He sulked, and Cousin Jenny laughed at him.

There was a lovely big garden to play in, and Jenny had a little bicycle and a tricycle too, so they had some fine racing. There was a swing to swing on and a sandpit to play in, so there was always plenty to do.

"Remember to bring in your toys when you come in!" Auntie Betty said. Jenny always remembered and Alan always forgot! Then out he had to go and collect them all.

"Remember to shut the gate when

you go out in case the puppy runs out and gets run over," said Auntie Betty, each morning. And again, Jenny always remembered, and Alan always forgot!

Auntie Betty was cross then. "Don't you *like* the puppy, Alan?" she would say. "Don't you care enough for the little thing to remember to shut the gate? You are unkind!"

"I *do* like him," said Alan. "I love him. He's a darling and I do love the way he wags his tail and comes running to meet me. I *will* remember to shut the gate."

"If anything happens to Paddy because of you, I'll never, never forgive you!" said Cousin Jenny. "You don't even *try* to remember things! I think you must have a very poor sort of brain."

"I *haven't*!" said Alan, at once. "My mother says I'm going to be clever. I've nearly been top at school three times!"

"Well, you're not clever *now!*" said Jenny. "Who left his toys out in the rain yesterday again? Who didn't . . ."

"Be quiet!" said Alan, sulkily. "I tell you I'm going to remember everything from now on!"

Certainly that day he was quite good at remembering all he had been told. He even remembered to shut the door quietly after him instead of slamming it. Auntie Betty was surprised!

"We shall send you back home a different boy!" she said. "Your mother will be pleased!"

Jenny and Alan were sent out next day to buy a collar and a lead for little Paddy the pup.

"He's growing now," said Auntie Betty. "He must learn to wear a collar, and to walk nicely on the lead."

"Can I take him out for a walk and teach him?" said Jenny. "Do let me!"

"Well – you're a very sensible little girl, so perhaps I'll let you!" said her mother.

"Can *I* take Paddy too?" asked Alan at

once. "I'm sensible as well."

"You're not," said Jenny. "You'd lose Paddy or let him get run over or something! He can't be trusted with Paddy, can he, Mummy?"

"We'll see," said her mother. "Anyway, you go and buy him a collar and lead this morning."

Paddy wasn't very pleased with his new collar, and he didn't like the lead at all! When Jenny put it on him and tried to walk him round the garden, he pulled away from her, and tried to escape.

"Oh, Paddy – you're nearly pulling my arm out!" said Jenny. "Walk to heel, and don't drag in front all the time."

"Let *me* take him," said Alan. "I'm a boy and boys' arms are stronger than girls'! I can soon teach him."

It was true that Alan was very good with Paddy. He was very patient and kind, and soon the puppy began to understand what it was that he was supposed to do.

"There you are!" boasted Alan. "I told you I could soon teach him!"

And then, at that very moment, Paddy gave a sudden jerk at the lead, pulled it out of Alan's hand, and ran to the front gate, where he had just seen a doggy friend pass by. The gate was open and the puppy frisked out into the road. A car hooted suddenly and swerved.

"Oh Paddy! He's out in the road!" cried Jenny and ran to get him. Her mother heard the car's hoot and looked out of the window. She was cross when she saw the puppy in the road.

"Who left that front gate open?" she called. And, of course, as usual it was Alan. He went very red in the face. "I did. I'm so sorry. I just came running in and swung it behind me, thinking it would shut all right," he said.

Jenny was hugging the puppy, glaring at her cousin angrily. "He nearly got run over! All because of you! Do you know what I would have done if he had been hurt? I would have thrown all your toys out of the window, and smashed your engine, and I would have told your mother to fetch you home, and – "

"That's enough, Jenny," said her mother. "You may be sure that if Alan does anything really bad *I* will deal with him and take him home, not you! Please do try and keep your temper!"

"I've said I was sorry, Jenny," said Alan.

"It isn't *enough* to be sorry – always to be sorry, sorry, sorry!" cried Jenny. "Why can't you be sensible? Then you wouldn't *have to be sorry!*"

Alan really did try to remember everything properly for the next two days. He was very good with the puppy too, and taught him a great deal. In fact, Paddy was soon walking beautifully on the lead, his nose just touching Alan's heels as he padded along.

"I can take Paddy for a walk, Mummy says," said Jenny next day. "Not with you. Only by myself."

"Oh, well, can *I* take him for a walk too, by *myself*?" said Alan. "Auntie, can I?"

"Yes," said his Aunt. "Jenny can take him this morning and you can take him this afternoon."

Jenny took Paddy off proudly, the lead fastened to his nice new collar. When she came back she told her mother that Paddy hadn't *really* been very good.

"He kept wanting to talk to all the other dogs he met," she said. "And sometimes I had to *drag* him away, and that's bad for his neck."

"You could have carried him then," said Alan. "That's what *I* shall do if I have any bother with him this afternoon. But I think he'll be very good with me."

Alan set out with Paddy after dinner. The little dog was delighted to have another walk. He trotted off at Alan's heels, as good as gold.

Alan talked to him all the way and

Paddy listened. "When you are with two-legged people, you don't stop and talk to *four*-legged creatures," Alan explained to him. "That's bad manners. But if *I* stop and talk, you just sit down politely and wait."

Paddy listened and behaved very well indeed. Then he suddenly pricked up his ears, and so did Alan. "Drums! Trumpets! There's a band coming!" he said. "I'll just tie you to this railing, Paddy, and go and stand at the kerb and watch. Sit there, like a good dog!"

Alan ran to the kerb to see the band pass. Rum-tiddy-rum, BOOM-BOOM-BOOM, tan-tan-tan-tara, BOOM! It was a wonderful band, and not only the soldiers were marching in time, but all the passers-by too! Some children came along, marching in a row, and called to Alan.

"Come on – this is fun!"

Alan joined in, and marched with the others, left-right, left-right, boom-diddy-boom, diddy-diddy-boom, boom, BOOM!

He went all the way with the soldiers till they came to their camp and went in through the gate. Then he turned to go home.

But before he had gone very far he remembered something. "Oh – PADDY! I left him tied up. Goodness me – I forgot all about him. Poor little puppy!"

He raced back to the railings to untie the puppy – but to his horror Paddy was gone. Alan stood and stared and then he looked up and down the road. Somebody must have stolen Paddy! He couldn't have got free by himself!

He ran to a woman standing outside a greengrocer's shop, serving her customers. "Oh please – did you see anyone take a puppy away a few minutes ago? He was tied to those railings."

"A puppy? Yes, I heard him whining," said the woman. "And when I looked

round I saw a girl taking his lead from the railing-spike, and leading him away."

"Oh! The wicked girl!" cried Alan. "What was she like? I'll go and tell a policeman!"

"Well — she seemed quite ordinary," said the woman, surprised. "She had on a blue dress with yellow stripes and a blue hat with yellow flowers, and sandals. That's all I remember."

Alan saw a policeman standing at a nearby corner and ran to him. "Please!" he said. "Someone's stolen my puppy. I left him over there for a minute — and a girl in a blue dress with yellow stripes took him away."

"Now, don't you upset yourself," said the policeman, opening his notebook. "Give me your name and address, and the dog's name — and I'll soon make enquiries. Don't you worry!"

Alan felt dreadful. How could he have forgotten little Paddy? Jenny was right, he must have a poor sort of brain.

He loved Paddy. He couldn't bear to think anything had happened to him. Whatever would Jenny say – and Auntie Betty?

"Jenny said she'd throw all my things out of the window!" he remembered. "She said she'd tell my mother and I'd be sent home. How can I go and say I've lost Paddy? I daren't. I simply daren't!"

He decided to go back to his aunt's, slip in at the back door, and go up to pack his things. He would go home to his mother and tell her what a failure he was – he had even lost the puppy he loved! He wouldn't tell Jenny and his aunt what had happened – he wouldn't even see them.

He ran back to the house and slipped in at the back door. No one was about. He went upstairs, found all his toys and clothes and packed them into his bag. Then he crept downstairs, meaning to catch the bus.

And *just* as he tried to slip out of the back door, who should come in but his aunt! How surprised she was to see Alan stealing out with his suitcase!

"Why — whatever are you doing? Where are you going?" she said. And then Alan burst into tears, though he knew it was a babyish thing to do.

"I lost Paddy!" he wailed. "I tied him to a railing and followed a band, and forgot him. And when I got back he wasn't there. A girl came and stole him!"

"Oh, Alan!" said his aunt.

"I told a policeman!" said Alan, wiping his eyes. "I hope he'll put that girl into prison. She's wicked. But I'm wicked too, to forget Paddy."

Suddenly there came a knock at the front door. Auntie Betty went to open it. Outside stood the policeman — and with him were Jenny — and Paddy! A most excited Paddy who flung himself on Alan at once and licked him all over.

"Why — what's this!" said Auntie Betty.

"Mother, this policeman stopped me and said Paddy wasn't mine!" cried Jenny. "I suddenly saw him tied up to a railing all by himself, and he was whining so loudly that I couldn't bear it. Alan wasn't anywhere about – so I guessed he had forgotten Paddy and I untied him and took him shopping with me."

"Er – well – it seems that a bit of a mistake has been made," said the policeman, smiling. "Ah, there's the boy who reported to me that the dog was stolen – stolen by a girl in a blue dress with yellow stripes, he said – so, of course, when I saw this young lady dressed like that, *and* with a dog, well, I had to find out what was happening!"

"You'd better take that boy to prison!" said Jenny, pointing at poor Alan. "He's a bad, wicked boy!"

"Don't be silly, Jenny," said her mother. She thanked the policeman, then said goodbye to him and shut the front door. "Look – Alan is so upset about everything that he has packed his bag and wants to go home. Shall we let him?"

Jenny stared at Alan's red eyes, and watched Paddy trying to comfort him. "I shan't ever forget things again – not after this," said Alan, in a low voice, stroking Paddy's soft head. "If you could just trust me once more . . ."

"All right," said Jenny. "I'll forgive you – but only because Paddy does, see? I don't *really* want you to go home."

So Alan unpacked his bag again and stayed. "You've taught me a lesson, Paddy," he told the puppy. "I've taught *you* plenty of things – and you learnt them well. Now you've taught *me* something, and I'll learn that well too. Do you understand?"

"Wuff!" said Paddy. Yes – of *course* he understood!

# The little thimble-plant

Natalie was very good at sewing. "It's in the family!" her mother told her. "Your great-granny embroidered so beautifully that the Queen of England bought some of her work. And you know how well your granny sews."

"Yes – and so do you, Mummy!" said Natalie. "I'm sure no one can make dresses as well as you can!"

Natalie had a beautiful silver thimble. Her great-granny had used it, and her granny had given it to Natalie when she saw that her little granddaughter was going to sew beautifully.

"Here you are," she said. "My mother used it when she embroidered the tablecloth that the Queen bought. You shall have it. She always said that it had magic in it, because she never sewed so well as when she wore that little thimble!"

Natalie always used the silver thimble. It fitted her middle finger exactly, and shone brightly as she pushed the needle in and out of her work. She often wondered if there really *was* magic in it!

Natalie was fond of gardening as well as sewing. She embroidered flowers on cushions, and she loved to copy her own flowers with her needle and coloured cottons. She had the prettiest little garden, full of candytuft, poppies, marigolds and roses.

"You must go in for the flower show this year," her mother said. "Do you know what the prize in the children's section is, Natalie? It's a work-basket! You need a new one, a nice big one. Wouldn't it be lovely if you could win the prize and take home a big new work-basket!"

"Oh, *yes*," said Natalie, delighted. "I'll grow some lovely flowers in my garden and take them to the show. Is the work-basket to be awarded for any special flowers, Mummy?"

"It's for the prettiest and most unusual plant that is flowering in a pot," said her mother. "You could put one of your garden plants into a pot and show that. You have one or two really unusual poppies. Those double red ones with pink stripes are the prettiest I have ever seen. You would be sure to win a prize with those."

Natalie took her sewing into the garden and sat down by her little garden. She looked at it as she sewed. As Mummy said, those red poppies striped curiously with pink might win a prize.

"It really would be fun to bring home that work-basket," said Natalie to herself. "Now, I'll just finish this bit of sewing, then I'll water my garden. It looks very dry."

She finished her sewing, left it on the grass and went to water her garden. The thirsty earth drank up the water thankfully. Natalie pulled up a few weeds, then gathered up her sewing things and went indoors.

But that evening, when she was showing her mother her sewing, she missed her little silver thimble! "Oh dear – where is it?" she said, hunting in her sewing-bag. "Oh, Mummy, I must have left it out on the grass. I'll have to go and look for it. It's still light."

So out she went. But although she hunted through every blade of grass by her garden she couldn't find her silver thimble. She went back to the house, upset.

"It's gone," she said. "Mummy, could anyone have taken it? Nobody comes into the garden, do they? I'm sure I left it down by my garden. But it isn't there now."

Mummy went to look too, and then they turned out the sewing-bag again.

They hunted all over the floor, and down the garden path. But the silver thimble didn't turn up. Natalie was worried.

"Oh, Mummy, I'm sure that was my lucky thimble. I do hope my good luck won't go now I've lost Granny's magic thimble. She always said it had magic in it. I'm sure it had, too. I could always do my best sewing when I was wearing that."

Well, it was a very strange thing, but it did seem as if Natalie's good luck disappeared with her silver thimble. First she fell off her bicycle and hurt her right hand so that she couldn't sew for a week. Then the dog got hold of the new cushion cover she was making for her mother and bit a hole in it. Then she lost one of her school books and got a scolding.

"If only I could find my silver thimble, I'm sure I'd be lucky again," she told her mother.

"Oh, nonsense," said Mummy. "It's

nothing to do with your thimble. Everyone has bad luck at times. I expect yours has finished now. You'll get a bit of good luck instead!"

But her mother was wrong. Three days before the flower show, just when Natalie's garden was looking really beautiful, two sheep wandered in at the back gate and ran all over the lawns and beds. One found its way into Natalie's garden and ate almost every plant in it!

Natalie ran crying to her mother. "Mummy! There's more bad luck! Those sheep, look – one has eaten nearly everything in my garden. My beautiful poppies – I can't possibly enter them for the flower show now. I haven't a chance now of winning that lovely work-basket!"

Mummy was very sad for her. She shook her head when she saw the spoilt garden. The sheep had been chased back to their field – but oh, what a lot of damage they had done! What a pity to spoil all Natalie's lovely flowers!

"Poor Natalie," said Mummy. "Never mind, darling. Nasty things do happen. You just have to make up your mind not to be upset too much. I've always noticed that if you make the best of bad things, something good comes along sooner or later!"

Natalie was very sad. She took her sewing down by her poor spoilt garden and began to embroider poppies on a new cushion-cover. "And if the dog gets this one I really will shout at him!" she thought. "Oh dear – I've got to use this horrid little pink thimble instead of my own lovely silver one. *Where* did it go, I wonder? Is somebody else wearing it now?"

A little robin hopped down beside her to watch her. Natalie called him *her* robin because he always came to watch when she gardened. She spoke to him and he cocked his head on one side, listening.

"I'm sad because my luck has

disappeared with my little silver thimble," she told him. "I did love it so. Robin, *you* haven't seen it, have you? Do you know who has got it? Did it go down a worm-hole – and is the worm using it for a hat?"

That idea made her laugh. The robin listened, and then gave a sudden little trill and flew into the nearby hedge. She heard him singing loudly, almost as if he were telling somebody something. Natalie wished she could understand what he was singing.

And then a most surprising thing happened. Out from the tangle of weeds in the hedge peeped a small face with bright green eyes, and a very long beard. The face wore a pointed hat on its head, and it looked rather worried.

Natalie stared in surprise. Was it a doll? No, it couldn't be – the face was too small. Besides, it moved. It smiled! And then the face moved forward and a whole body appeared, as somebody came through the weeds.

It was a brownie — such a small brownie that Natalie thought he could live in her doll's house with ease. He came right up to her, the robin fluttering behind.

"You're Natalie, aren't you?" said the brownie, his long beard waving round him in the breeze. "The robin told me. And he said you've lost your silver thimble and you're very upset."

"Yes. I loved it," said Natalie. "Do you know where it is? And are you a brownie? I've seen pictures of brownies in my books, but I never thought that one lived just under my hedge!"

"Children aren't as kind to little creatures as they should be," said the brownie. "So we hide away now. But we're always about. The robin told me you were kind, so I'm not afraid to come and speak to you. And I'm really very, very sorry — but I'm afraid *I've* got your thimble. At least, I think it must be what you call a thimble, though I've never used one myself."

"But why did you take it?" asked Natalie gently, afraid of scaring him.

"I found it halfway down a worm-hole," said the brownie. "I heard the worm complaining because he couldn't get out. It was stopping up his way, you see. So I dragged it out and took it home. I didn't know it belonged to you."

"What did you do with it?" asked Natalie, feeling really excited.

"Well, to tell the truth, I thought it was a plant pot," said the brownie. "Silly of me – but I honestly thought it was. So I planted a seed in it to grow and stood it on a little wooden stand on my window-sill. I'll let you have it back at once, of course."

"Oh, please do!" said Natalie, delighted. "I don't mind your having had it for a plant pot at all – if only you'll give it back to me now. I'll give you this little *pink* thimble if you like, for a plant pot."

"Now that's *very* kind of you," said the brownie, and darted off at once.

He came back with Natalie's silver thimble. He carried it upside down, of course, fitted into its stand because to him it was a pot. In it grew a tiny plant with pretty, feathery leaves.

"What have you planted in my thimble?" asked Natalie.

"It's a wing-flower," said the brownie. "Its flowers are just like fairy-wings, you know, in fact, some fairies cut them off and use them for a spare pair. They only need a spell in them to make them fly."

Natalie looked down at the tiny plant in wonder. It had a nice fat bud at the top! Would it flower into tiny fairy-wings? Oh, how wonderful!

"Thank you. I shan't take out this magic little plant till it dies," said Natalie. "Fancy, it's so small that it grows in a thimble! I shall wait and see if it flowers into wings. Look, here is my pink thimble for you. Come and talk to me again sometime. I'll send the robin to call you when I am here all alone."

"I'd like that," said the green-eyed fellow, and nodded his head. "Thank you for the pink thimble. *I* think it's prettier than the other. Goodbye!"

Natalie took the thimble-plant to her mother. How marvellous! What a wonderful thing to happen!

Mummy could really hardly believe it. She looked closely at the tiny plant. "I have *never* seen one like it before," she said. "Oh, Natalie, you ought to show it at the flower show! It's quite perfect. It should be in flower then, too!"

Well, on the day of the flower show the little thimble-plant burst into flower – and to Natalie's great delight the flower was in the shape of fairy-wings, two dainty blue and silver wings, quivering on the stalk.

"It *is* a wing-flower," said Natalie. "Oh, Mummy, if only I was small enough to fly with them! When the flower dies I'll cut off the wings and fasten them to a little dolls' house doll – *she* might fly with them at night!"

She took the thimble-plant to the show. Everyone exclaimed in wonder when they saw such a strange little plant, with tiny wings quivering at the top of the stalk.

"Wonderful! Marvellous! Where did you get it from?"

Natalie whispered her tale to the children, but she didn't think the grown-ups would believe her, so she didn't say anything to them. The children crowded round the thimble-plant, holding their breath in case they damaged the fairy-wings growing at the top.

Well, of course, you can guess who got the prize. Natalie! She would have got the prize for her poppies, if she had shown them, so she really only got what she deserved. But how pleased she was! Mummy carried the big work-basket home for her, and Natalie carefully carried the strange little plant growing from her silver thimble.

She cut off the wings when the flower

seemed dead, though they were still exactly like proper little wings. And, at the foot of the flower, was a tiny ball of seeds – seeds so fine that they seemed almost like powder.

I wish Natalie would give me one. I *would* so love to grow a wing-flower in a silver thimble, wouldn't you?

## The little brownies' race

"Now come along, come along, come along!" shouted Old Man Smarty. "Where are you, Shuffle, Trot and Merry? I've some goods here ready for you to take to my house!"

Shuffle, Trot and Merry, the three little brownies, were playing a game of marbles in a corner of the market. Shuffle groaned. "Blow! Now we must take his sacks on our backs and walk for miles to his house. I'm tired of it! Why doesn't he give us horses to ride?"

"Because we're cheaper than horses," said Trot. "Come along."

The three little fellows went along to where Old Man Smarty was standing by three big sacks.

"Oh – so there you are, you lazy lot!" he said. "Now see – I've bought all these things at the market, and I want them taken to my house as fast as possible, because Lord High-Up is sending for them tonight, and will pay me a good price."

"It's too hot to walk fast with big sacks like those!" said Shuffle.

"We shan't get there before midnight," said Trot, gloomily.

"Well – I'll do my best," said Merry.

"I'll give a gold piece to the one who gets to my house first," said Old Man Smarty. "There's generosity for you!"

Trot, Shuffle and Merry pricked up their ears at that! A gold piece! That was riches to them.

Sly old Shuffle went over to the sacks at once, and quickly felt them all. Ooh – what a heavy one – and the second was heavy too – but the third one felt as light as a feather! That was the one for him!

"I shall hardly know I've a sack on my

back!" he thought. "I shall easily be the first one at the master's house, and I shall get the gold piece before either of them is in sight! Oho – I'm clever, I am!"

He shuffled off with the very light sack on his back. Then Trot went over to the two sacks left, and wondered what was in them. He stuck a finger into one – it was full of something round and hard – potatoes, perhaps? He stuck a finger into the other and felt something loose and soft – what was it – flour – salt – sugar? He pulled out his finger and sucked it.

"Ah – *sugar*!" he said. "That's fine! I can cut a tiny hole in the sack and wet my finger and dip it into the sugar all the time I'm walking along. What a treat!"

So Trot took the second sack and set off to catch up with Shuffle. Merry whistled a jolly tune and went to the sack that was left. He made a face as he lifted it on to his back. "It's heavy – full of potatoes, I think – and the sellers haven't cleaned the mud off them, either, and that makes them twice as heavy. Well – here goes – I must catch up Shuffle and Trot before they get too far, or I'll not win that gold piece!"

But it was difficult to catch up with Shuffle, even though he was not the fastest walker as a rule – because his sack was so very, very light. Shuffle had no idea what was inside, and he didn't care. He was delighted to have picked such a light load!

"That gold piece is as good as in my pocket!" he thought to himself. "Instead of being last today I shall be first! And will I share that gold piece with the others? No, certainly not! They don't deserve it – I'm the sharpest of the lot!"

Trot was having quite a good time with his sack. He made a hole in it and as he trotted along he kept putting in his finger, getting it covered in sugar, and then licking it off. What a joke, he thought – he was lightening his load and having a feast at the same time!

Merry walked fast, but his load was really very heavy – and then he had the bad luck to stub his toe on a big stone, and that made him limp!

"Just my luck!" he groaned. "I always seem to get the heaviest load and to be last for some reason or other. Look at Shuffle now – he must have picked the lightest sack of the lot – and judging by the way Trot is poking his finger in and out of that sack, it's full of something nice to eat. Oh, my toe! I'll never get that gold piece. I can't walk fast with a sore toe!"

So Merry fell behind, but all the same he whistled a merry tune and had a joke for anyone he met.

Now very soon clouds began to cover the sun, and a wind blew up and made the trees sway to and fro. Then Merry felt a drop of rain on his face and he sighed.

"Now it's going to pour with rain and I shall get soaked. I'd better give up all hope of getting that gold piece!"

The rain began to pelt down, stinging the faces of the three little fellows with their sacks. Shuffle was a great way ahead of the others, and he grinned as he looked round and saw how distant Trot was. As for Merry, he was almost out of sight, he was so far behind.

But, as the rain poured down, queer things began to happen! First of all, Shuffle's sack became gradually heavier. He didn't notice it at first, and then he began to wonder.

"*Is* my sack getting heavy, or am I just imagining it?" he thought. He humped it over his shoulder and groaned. "My word, it feels twice as heavy! Whatever can be inside?"

He walked a little further and then felt that he must have a rest, for the sack was so terribly heavy. He set it down and undid the rope that tied the neck. He put in his hand and felt something soft and squashy. What could it be? The squashy thing was very wet indeed for the rain had penetrated right into the sack. Shuffle pulled it out and looked at it.

It was a sponge! A *sponge*! "No wonder the sack felt so light when the sponges were dry!" said Shuffle, in dismay. "Now they're soaked with rain water and as heavy as can be! What can I do?"

He took all the sponges out of the sack and squeezed them dry, and then began to put them back into the sack again. "But what's the use of that?" he groaned. "The rain is as heavy as ever, and the sponges will soon be full of water again!"

Trot came up and grinned. "Hello, Shuffle – so your load was sponges, was it? It serves you right for picking the lightest load as usual. Now you've got the heaviest!"

"What's in yours?" called Shuffle, annoyed, but Trot didn't stop. No, he saw a chance of winning that gold piece now. He was going quite fast. Also, his sack felt lighter!

In fact, it soon felt so light that Trot stopped in surprise. "What's happening to my sack?" he thought. "It really does feel remarkably light!"

He set it down to see – and, to his horror, he found that the sugar was all melting in the rain! The raindrops had soaked through the sack and the sugar was dissolving into sweetened water – and dripping fast out of the bottom of the sack!

"I ought to get under cover, or it will all be melted away," thought Trot, in dismay. "Why wasn't I sensible enough to remember that sugar melts? I *knew* it was sugar all right! Well, I've outpaced old Shuffle – but if I wait till the rain stops Merry will be sure to catch me up and pass me, and I shan't get that gold piece."

So on he went in the pouring rain, while the sugar in his sack melted faster than ever. But at least he was now in the lead!

As for Merry he still whistled in the

pouring rain, for he was a light-hearted
fellow. The rain ran into his sack, down
among the potatoes and soon muddy
water was dripping out at the bottom.
Merry laughed.

"You're washing all the dirty potatoes
for me!" he said to the rain clouds above.
"Hello – there's Shuffle in front of me –
he's very slow today!"

He soon passed Shuffle, who groaned
loudly as Merry passed him. "My load is
sponges!" he shouted. "And they're four
times as heavy as they were now that
they're soaked with rain."

"Serves you right!" said Merry. "You
picked the lightest sack so that you
could win that gold piece!"

The three went on through the rain,
and at last came one by one to Old Man
Smarty's big house. Trot went round to
the back door first of all and set down
his sack on the ground.

"Ha!" said the big cook, "so you've
brought something for the master, have
you? Well, wait till he calls you in to see

him. I'll tell him you were the first."

The next was Merry with his sack of potatoes. The cook peered at them and smiled. "Well I never – the potatoes are all washed clean for me! That's a good mark for you, Merry. Wait here till the master sends for you."

Last of all came poor Shuffle, very weary with carrying such a wet and heavy load. He set his sack down and water ran all over the floor.

"Now pick up that sack and stand it outside!" said the cook. "My floor's in enough mess already without you making it a running river. What in the world have you got in that sack?"

But Shuffle was too tired to answer. The cook gave them all some food and drink and they sat back and waited to take their sacks to the master.

The call came at last, and the cook took them in to Old Man Smarty.

"Here's the first one – he came before the others," she said, pushing Trot forward. His sack looked limp, wet and empty. Old Man Smarty glared at it.

"What's this? It should be full of sugar! Where's the sugar, Trot? Have you sold it to someone on the way?"

"No, sir. It was the rain that melted it," said Trot. "I was first here, sir. Can I have my gold piece?"

"Bah!" said Old Man Smarty. "Why didn't you get under cover and save my expensive sugar?" Then he turned to Shuffle. "Shuffle, you were third, so you're out of it. Take that disgusting, dripping sack out of the room. Merry, what about you?"

"Sir, he's brought potatoes – and they're all washed clean!" said the cook, eagerly, for she liked Merry. "He *deserves* the gold piece, even though he wasn't the first here!"

"*I* was first!" said Trot. "*I* won the gold. Give it to me, Old Man Smarty!"

"Very well – but *you* must pay me *two* gold pieces for all the sugar you've lost out of my sack," said Old Man Smarty. "That's what it cost me! So if I give you one gold piece, you have to give me two."

"All right. I won't claim it," said Trot, sulkily. "I should have got the sack under cover." He stamped out of the room in a rage. Only Merry was left.

"You weren't the first," said Old Man Smarty. "But you certainly delivered my goods in a better condition than when I bought them – so I shall award the gold piece for that."

He tossed a shining coin to the delighted Merry, who went off to the kitchen with his sack of potatoes. What sulks and grumbles met him from Shuffle and Trot! He clapped them on the shoulder. "Cheer up – we'll go and spend my gold piece together. What's good luck for but to be shared!"

They all went out arm in arm and the cook stared after them. "You deserve your good luck, Merry!" she called. "And what's more, you'll always get it – a merry face and a generous heart are the luckiest things in the world!"

# Nobody came to tea

There was once a lonely hare. He hadn't any friends, and he wanted some.

He talked to the scarecrow in the field, and the scarecrow gave him some advice.

"Ask people to tea. They like that. That is what children do. Give a party sometime, and ask all the creatures to come."

It was summer-time when the scarecrow told the hare this. The hare felt excited. "It will take me a long time to get things for the party," he said. "I will ask everyone for the last week in October. Then I shall have plenty of time to collect food for my guests."

He asked the little dormouse, who was delighted. He asked the prickly hedgehog, and he was very pleased. He asked both the frog and the toad, and as they were cousins they said they would come together.

"That's four," said the hare. "Now, who's next to be asked? Oh yes – I'll ask the lizard and the snake, and I'll ask the little black bat too. He will enjoy a party. I must try to get some beetles for him."

So he asked them all, and they said yes, they would all come to tea with him and be friends.

"Seven guests," the hare told the scarecrow. "It's a *real* party, isn't it?"

Well, the day of the party came. The hare had collected food for every one of his guests, and he set it all out in his field.

Then he waited for his visitors to come. But nobody came to tea. Nobody at all. The dormouse didn't turn up, and neither did the hedgehog. The frog and

toad were not to be seen. The lizard didn't come frisking along, and no gliding, silent snake came to tea. Even the little black bat was missing too.

The hare was sad. "Nobody likes me," he said. "Nobody has come to tea. They said they would – but they were making fun of me. They didn't mean to come."

"What's the matter?" said the rabbit, who was passing by. The hare told him. The rabbit laughed loudly.

"Silly hare! The dormouse is down at the bottom of the ivy-roots, asleep. The hedgehog is snoring in a hole in the bank over there. The frog is at the bottom of the pond, and the toad asleep under a stone. The lizard is in a hollow stump, and the snake sleeps with his brothers in an old tree. The little black bat is asleep too, hanging upside down in the barn."

"Asleep! Why are they all asleep?" said the hare.

"Well, they always sleep the winter away – didn't you know that?" said the rabbit scornfully. "It's no good having a party at this time of year. But cheer up – I and my family will come if you like. We shan't eat the tea you've got ready – but we'll all play games."

So they did, and the hare enjoyed himself after all. But none of his real guests came to the party – they wouldn't wake up till the spring-time.

# The bold, bad boys!

Derek and Tom loved to go down and play beside the river. They liked watching the boats go by, and when a steamer sailed along in midstream, making quite big waves break against the banks, they shouted with joy.

"Daddy, can't we have a boat of our own?" begged Derek. "Lots of the boys we know have. Why can't we?"

"For a very good reason," said Daddy. "You can't swim yet! I tried to teach you last summer, but you both cried because the water was cold, and Tom yelled when I held him up and tried to make him do the arm-strokes."

The two boys looked rather ashamed. "If you'd let us have a boat, we promise we will learn to swim this summer," said Derek.

"Oh, no!" said Daddy. "I'll promise you a boat when you have learnt to swim. That's the right way to put it."

The boys went off, rather sulky. "Lots of people who can't swim have boats," said Tom. "How can we have adventures, and go rowing off to find them, if we haven't got a boat. Daddy's mean."

"Never mind," said Derek. "We'll have a good time paddling. We'll call ourselves The Bold, Bad Boys and we'll look for adventures every single day. We'll be pirates and smugglers, and we'll be very bold and daring."

So they were. They became a great nuisance to the moorhens by the river, and the big swans hissed at them as they sailed grandly by. But when the cows came down to stand in the shallow part of the river, The Bold, Bad Boys ran away. They were rather afraid of cows!

Now, one day, when the two boys were sitting by the water, splashing it with their feet, they saw something coming down the river. It wasn't a boat. It wasn't a bird. What could it be?

"It's a barrel! An empty barrel, floating along by itself!" cried Derek. "If only we could get it, Tom. We could play smugglers properly if we had a barrel of our own! We could even hide in it."

They watched the barrel. It came bobbing along – and floated to where a low branch stretched out from the bank over the water. There it caught and stopped.

"Look, look!" cried Derek. "That branch has caught it. Oh, Tom, let's be really bold and crawl out on that branch and get the barrel. I think the water is shallow there, and maybe we could get on the barrel and push it over to the bank."

So, feeling very bold and daring, the two boys crawled along the branch to the barrel. Derek leaned down and caught hold of it.

"Tom, can you get on to the barrel whilst I hold it?" he said. "Quick, in case I have to let go. That's right. Oh, good, you're riding the barrel! Will it take me too, do you think?"

Tom had dropped neatly on to the barrel, and was now riding it astride, grinning happily. Derek dropped down beside him.

Now they were both on the barrel. "Work hard with your feet and we'll get it to the bank," said Derek. But, alas, as soon as they left the tree branch, the barrel, instead of going towards the bank, got caught by the midstream current and swung out into deep water. Then it began floating merrily down the river with the two boys riding it!

Tom screamed. "Derek, Derek! We're out in deep water. We'll drown!"

"Not if we cling to the barrel," said Derek, going rather white. "Hold on, Tom. Don't let go whatever you do. Oh,

gracious, we're going fast!"

"I feel sick, I feel sick," wailed Tom. "I want to be rescued. Oooooooooh!"

Derek was scared, too. He clung to the bobbing barrel and looked round to see if any boat was about. Not one was anywhere to be seen. So on they bobbed and on and on.

Tom was crying.

Then suddenly a fisherman by the river saw them. "Help, help!" cried Derek. "Save us!"

In the greatest astonishment the fisherman ran to a small boat nearby and got into it. With three or four strong pulls at the oars he was soon alongside the barrel. He pulled the boys into the boat. Tom burst into wails.

"We were nearly drowned. Take me home to Mummy."

The fisherman rowed to shore. He found out where the boys lived and took them both back, wet and scared. Daddy came out when he saw them.

"Whatever's the matter?" he said.

"Have you fallen in the river?"

"No, oh no!" wailed Tom. "We saw a barrel floating down and we crawled out on a tree branch to it . . ."

"And got on it, meaning to take it to the bank, and it floated away with us," said Derek.

"I rescued them in time," said the fisherman, winking at Daddy. "Seems to me they're strange boys, not liking an adventure. Most boys are looking out for one every day."

"So do Tom and Derek," said their father. "In fact, I believe they call themselves The Bold, Bad Boys, and half the time they're smugglers and pirates. And when a little adventure like this comes along, they yell and howl and can't bear it! Well, well, well!"

"Why didn't they swim to shore?" asked the fisherman, surprised to hear all this.

"I'm sorry to have to tell you – but both boys are too scared to learn to swim," said Daddy, solemnly. "They want a boat – and yet they can't swim!"

"Well, they had a barrel for a boat, and they didn't seem to like that at all," said the fisherman. "I reckon a boat would be wasted on them, sir."

"Just what I think," said Daddy. "Well, thanks for rescuing them. Maybe one day they will welcome an adventure when they get one, instead of howling about it."

"Thanks for rescuing us, sir," said Derek, his face very red indeed. He felt so ashamed. To think they were the two Bold, Bad Boys, always looking out for an adventure, and now they had behaved like this!

Derek took Tom into the garden into their secret corner. "We're going to learn to swim!" he told Tom fiercely. "Do you hear, Tom? And there's to be no moaning and groaning about it. We're going to make Daddy proud of us for a change!"

Well, the last time I saw Derek and Tom they were in a small, neat boat of their own, rowing out on the river. So I knew they had learnt to swim, and could really look for exciting adventures. Do you know what they have called their boat? Guess! It's called *The Bold, Bad Boys*!